BEAR IN SUNSHINE

Written by Stella Blackstone
Illustrated by Debbie Harter

Barefoot Books
better books for children

Bear likes to play
when the sun shines,

Bear likes to sing in the rain.

He flies his red kite
when the wind blows,

When it's icy,
he skates in the lane.

Bear likes to paint
when it's misty,

When storms come, he hides in his bed.

When snow falls, he likes to make snow-bears,

Whatever the weather,
come snow, rain or sun,

Bear always knows how to have lots of fun!

Spring

Summer

Autumn

Winter

For Felix — S.B.
For Julia and Isabella — D.H.

Barefoot Books
PO Box 95
Kingswood
Bristol BS30 5BH

This book was typeset in Futura
The illustrations were prepared in watercolour, pen and ink and crayon on thick watercolour paper

Graphic design by Polka. Creation, Bath
Colour separation by Grafiscan, Verona
Printed and bound in Singapore by Tien Wah Press Pte Ltd

This book has been printed on 100% acid-free paper

Hardcover ISBN 1 84148 320 6
Paperback ISBN 1 84148 322 2

British Cataloguing-in-Publication Data: a catalogue record for this book
is available from the British Library

1 3 5 7 9 8 6 4 2

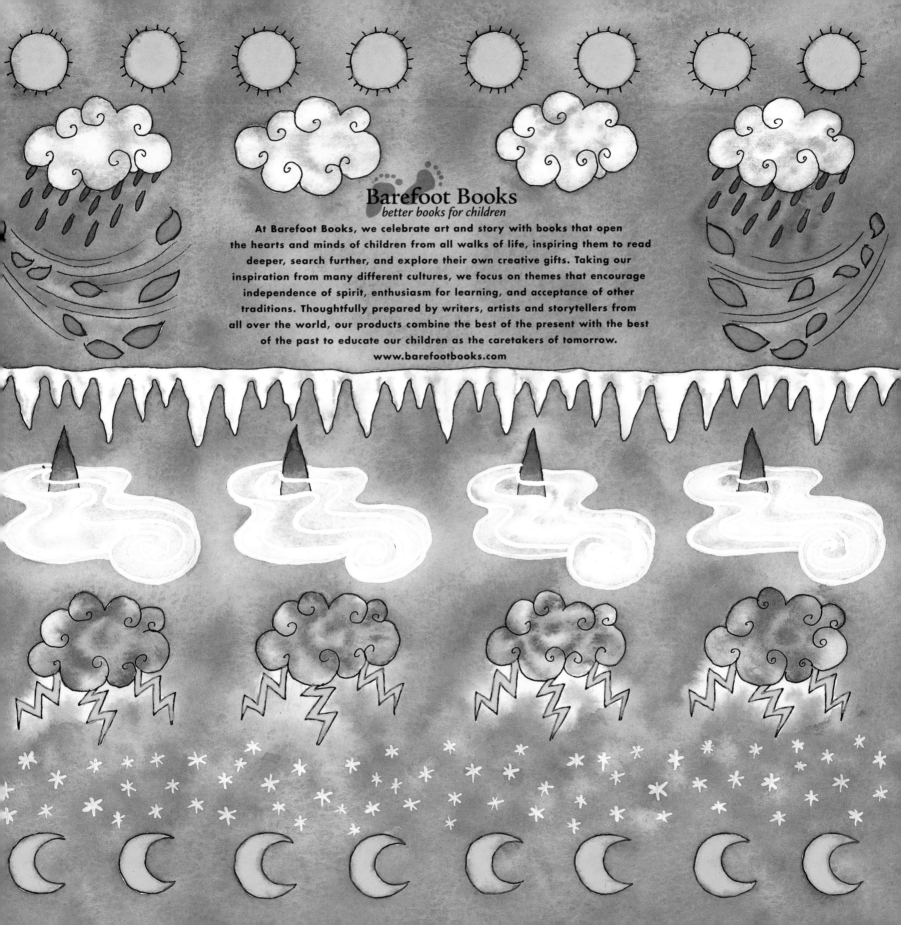

Barefoot Books
better books for children

At Barefoot Books, we celebrate art and story with books that open
the hearts and minds of children from all walks of life, inspiring them to read
deeper, search further, and explore their own creative gifts. Taking our
inspiration from many different cultures, we focus on themes that encourage
independence of spirit, enthusiasm for learning, and acceptance of other
traditions. Thoughtfully prepared by writers, artists and storytellers from
all over the world, our products combine the best of the present with the best
of the past to educate our children as the caretakers of tomorrow.
www.barefootbooks.com